This book should be returned to any branch of the
Lancashire County Library on or before the date shown

# The Busy Lunch

Level 2H

Written by Melanie Hamm
Illustrated by Stefania Maragna

# What is synthetic phonics?

**Synthetic phonics** teaches children to recognise the sounds of letters and to blend (synthesise) them together to make whole words.

Understanding sound/letter relationships gives children the confidence and ability to read unfamiliar words, without having to rely on memory or guesswork; this helps them progress towards independent reading.

**Did you know?** Spoken English uses more than 40 speech sounds. Each sound is called a *phoneme*. Some phonemes relate to a single letter (d-o-g) and others to combinations of letters (sh-ar-p). When a phoneme is written down it is called a *grapheme*. Teaching these sounds, matching them to their written form and sounding out words for reading is the basis of synthetic phonics.

# Consultant

*I love reading phonics* has been created in consultation with language expert Abigail Steel. She has a background in teaching and teacher training and is a respected expert in the field of Synthetic Phonics. Abigail Steel is a regular contributor to educational publications. Her international education consultancy supports parents and teachers in the promotion of literacy skills.

# Reading tips

This book focuses on the sounds from level 2:
sh, ch, th as in 'them', th as in 'thin', ng, nk, le

## Tricky words in this book

Any words in bold may have unusual spellings or are
new and have not yet been introduced.

Tricky words in this book:

### has the of no I we need goes to he wood chairs hay falls they says

## Extra ways to have fun with this book

After the reader has read the story, ask them questions
about what they have just read:

*What things did Rabbit forget he needed for lunch?*
*Why did Rabbit need a rest at the end of the story?*

Make flashcards of the focus graphemes. Ask the
reader to say the sounds. This will help
reinforce letter/sound matches.

'I'm going, they
wouldn't let me read
at the table.

# A pronunciation guide

This grid contains the sounds used in
the story and a guide on how to say them.

| | | | | |
|---|---|---|---|---|
| s<br>as in sat | a<br>as in ant | t<br>as in tin | p<br>as in pig | i<br>as in ink |
| n<br>as in net | c<br>as in cat | e<br>as in egg | h<br>as in hen | r<br>as in rat |
| m<br>as in mug | d<br>as in dog | g<br>as in get | o<br>as in ox | u<br>as in up |
| l<br>as in log | f<br>as in fan | b<br>as in bag | j<br>as in jug | v<br>as in van |
| w<br>as in wet | z<br>as in zip | y<br>as in yet | k<br>as in kit | qu<br>as in quick |
| x<br>as in box | ff<br>as in off | ll<br>as in ball | ss<br>as in kiss | zz<br>as in buzz |
| ck<br>as in duck | pp<br>as in puppy | nn<br>as in bunny | rr<br>as in arrow | gg<br>as in egg |
| dd<br>as in daddy | bb<br>as in chubby | tt<br>as in attic | sh<br>as in shop | ch<br>as in chip |
| th<br>as in them | th<br>as in thin | ng<br>as in sing | nk<br>as in sunk | le<br>as in bottle |

Be careful not to add an 'uh' sound to 's', 't', 'p',
'c', 'h', 'r', 'm', 'd', 'g', 'l', 'f' and 'b'. For example,
say 'fff' not 'fuh' and 'sss' not 'suh'.

Rabbit **has** a den. Dog and Rat visit for lunch.

**The** den is full **of** things, a sink, a kettle, a rug, a jug, pots, pans and cups.

But Rabbit has **no** table!

"**I** forgot. **We need** a table!"

Dog **goes to** the shed. **He** gets
thick bits of **wood**. Dog chops it.

But Rabbit has no **chairs**!

"I forgot. We need chairs!"

Rat gets **hay** to sit on.

But Rabbit has no lunch!

"I forgot.
We need lunch!"

Then a leg **falls** off the table!

And bugs from the hay are in the den! Buzz! Buzz! Buzz!

Quick, get out of the den!

**They** have a picnic for lunch.

It is the best.

"I need a nap,"
**says** Rabbit.

"I forgot. I need a bed!"

Dog and Rat did not!

# OVER **48** TITLES IN SIX LEVELS
## Abigail Steel recommends...

### Other titles to enjoy from Level 2

I love reading phonics **Chuck and Duck**

978-1-84898-387-8

I love reading phonics **Let's go to the Swings**

978-1-84898-549-0

I love reading phonics **Wish Fish**

978-1-84898-386-1

### Some titles from Level 1

I love reading phonics **Bad Rat**

978-1-84898-277-2

I love reading phonics **The Best Gift**

978-1-84898-396-0

I love reading phonics **Clint and Grant Play I-Spy**

978-1-84898-548-3

I love reading phonics **Gran and Bret's Trip**

978-1-84898-547-6

### Some titles from Level 3

I love reading phonics **Bart's Go-Cart**

978-1-84898-552-0

I love reading phonics **Queen Ella's Feet**

978-1-84898-398-4

I love reading phonics **Puff Flies**

978-1-84898-399-1

I love reading phonics **The Pop Duet**

978-1-84898-551-3

An Hachette UK Company
www.hachette.co.uk

Copyright © Octopus Publishing Group Ltd 2012
First published in Great Britain in 2012 by TickTock, a division of Octopus Publishing Group Ltd,
Endeavour House, 189 Shaftesbury Avenue, London WC2H 8JY.
www.octopusbooks.co.uk

ISBN 978 1 84898 556 8

Printed and bound in China
10 9 8 7 6 5 4 3 2 1